Dear Parent:
Your child's love of reading starts here!

Every child learns to read in a different way and at his or her own speed. Some go back and forth between reading levels and read favorite books again and again. Others read through each level in order. You can help your young reader improve and become more confident by encouraging his or her own interests and abilities. From books your child reads with you to the first books he or she reads alone, there are I Can Read Books for every stage of reading:

SHARED READING
Basic language, word repetition, and whimsical illustrations, ideal for sharing with your emergent reader

BEGINNING READING
Short sentences, familiar words, and simple concepts for children eager to read on their own

READING WITH HELP
Engaging stories, longer sentences, and language play for developing readers

READING ALONE
Complex plots, challenging vocabulary, and high-interest topics for the independent reader

ADVANCED READING
Short paragraphs, chapters, and exciting themes for the perfect bridge to chapter books

I Can Read Books have introduced children to the joy of reading since 1957. Featuring award-winning authors and illustrators and a fabulous cast of beloved characters, I Can Read Books set the standard for beginning readers.

A lifetime of discovery begins with the magical words **"I Can Read!"**

Visit www.icanread.com for information
on enriching your child's reading experience.

Digger the Dinosaur
Copyright © 2011 by HarperCollins Publishers
All rights reserved. Manufactured in the United States of America. No part of this book may be used or reproduced in any manner whatsoever
without written permission except in the case of brief quotations embodied in critical articles and reviews. For information address
HarperCollins Children's Books, a division of HarperCollins Publishers, 10 East 53rd Street, New York, NY 10022.
www.icanread.com
Book design by Tom Starace
Library of Congress Cataloging-in-Publication Data is available.
ISBN 978-0-06-222222-0 (trade bdg.) — ISBN 978-0-06-222221-3 (pbk.)

13 14 15 16 17   LP/WOR   10 9 8 7 6 5 4 3 2   ❖   First print edition

I Can Read!™

SHARED
My First
READING

Digger the Dinosaur

by Rebecca Kai Dotlich
pictures by Gynux

HARPER
An Imprint of HarperCollinsPublishers

Digger was a good dinosaur.
But he was a busy dinosaur.
Sometimes he forgot to listen.

"Digger!" Momasaur called.
"Clean your room."

Digger looked at Stego.

Stego looked at Digger.

"Can't I play?" Digger asked.

"No," said Momasaur.

"Your room is a mess."

"She said yes?" asked Digger.

"She said MESS," said Stego.

"I can fix that," said Digger.

"I will help!" said Stego.
"Let's go!" said Digger.

9

"Put your coat on the hook,"
said Stego.
So Digger did.

"Digger!" said Stego.

"You put your coat on a BOOK."

"You said book," said Digger.

"I said HOOK," said Stego.

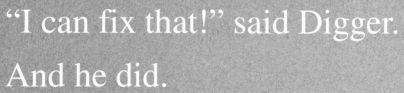

"I can fix that!" said Digger.
And he did.

13

"Let's put these bones away,"
said Stego.

So Digger did.
And Stego did.

"Digger!" said Stego.

"You put the STONES away!"

"You said stones," said Digger.

"I said BONES," said Stego.

"I can fix that," said Digger.

And he did.

Momasaur walked in.
"Put those hats away,"
she said, "and then go play."

"Hurry!" said Digger.

And he did.

And Stego did.

20

"Wait!" said Digger.

"Did she say HATS?"

Stego nodded. "I think so."

21

Digger and Stego roared.
"We both got mixed up!"
said Stego.

Momasaur walked in.

"Good job," she said.

"No more mess!"

"She said yes!" said Digger.
"Let's play ball!"
And they did.